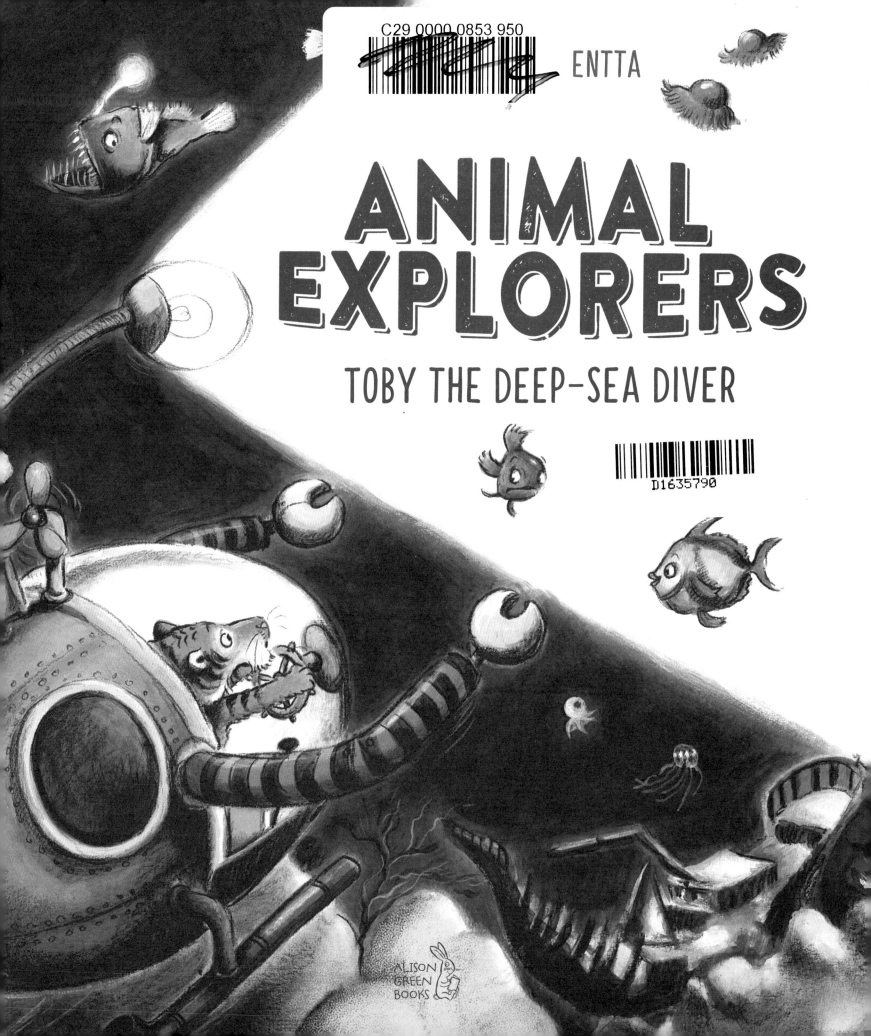

ENTTA

ANIMAL EXPLORERS

TOBY THE DEEP-SEA DIVER

ALISON
GREEN
BOOKS

Toby wasn't quite like the other tigers. While they swam, Toby dived, right down under the water. **"Tigers don't dive!"** said his mum. But Toby couldn't understand why. There was so much to see.

There were things with fins,

things with **tentacles,**

there were
even things with
wings!

But what Toby really wanted to know was what lived down in the Deep: the pitch-black bottom of the ocean where no tiger had ever been. He read lots of books. He told his mum fascinating facts.

Did you know the ocean is deeper than Mount Everest?

Some weird fish have lamps on their heads!

But he still wanted to know more.
At last Mum gave Toby his
very own scuba-diving kit.
Now he could do lots
more exploring.

Wetsuits are really tight!

But now Toby could dive all
over his local coral reef.

It was packed with colourful creatures,
and he took loads of pictures with
his underwater camera.

He'd seen seahorses,
cuttlefish, stingrays,
eels . . .

Seahorses

Moray eel

Cuttlefish

Stingrays

Octopus

. . . and an octopus!

But he still longed to go to the Deep.
Toby despaired. It was far too deep for a tiger to dive.

Then he had an idea.

He'd heard about
a bison who could make
anything out of the rubbish that
people throw away. Toby needed a
submersible: a mini submarine
that could take him right
down into the Deep.

If anyone could make one, it was Bison.

Toby helped him pick out some useful bits and pieces.

Then they hammered and bashed and tinkered,

and scratched their heads until . . .

. . . they'd done it!

"That," said Bison, "is a magnificent submersible."
Toby's mum was very impressed, too. Toby promised
her that he'd drive carefully, and be back in time for tea.

Now all he had to do was launch the sub in the water, learn how to steer, and work out how to use the grabber arms.

How hard could it be?

Well, harder than it looked. He spent a lot of time upside down.

But after **lots** of practice
he was ready to head to the Deep.

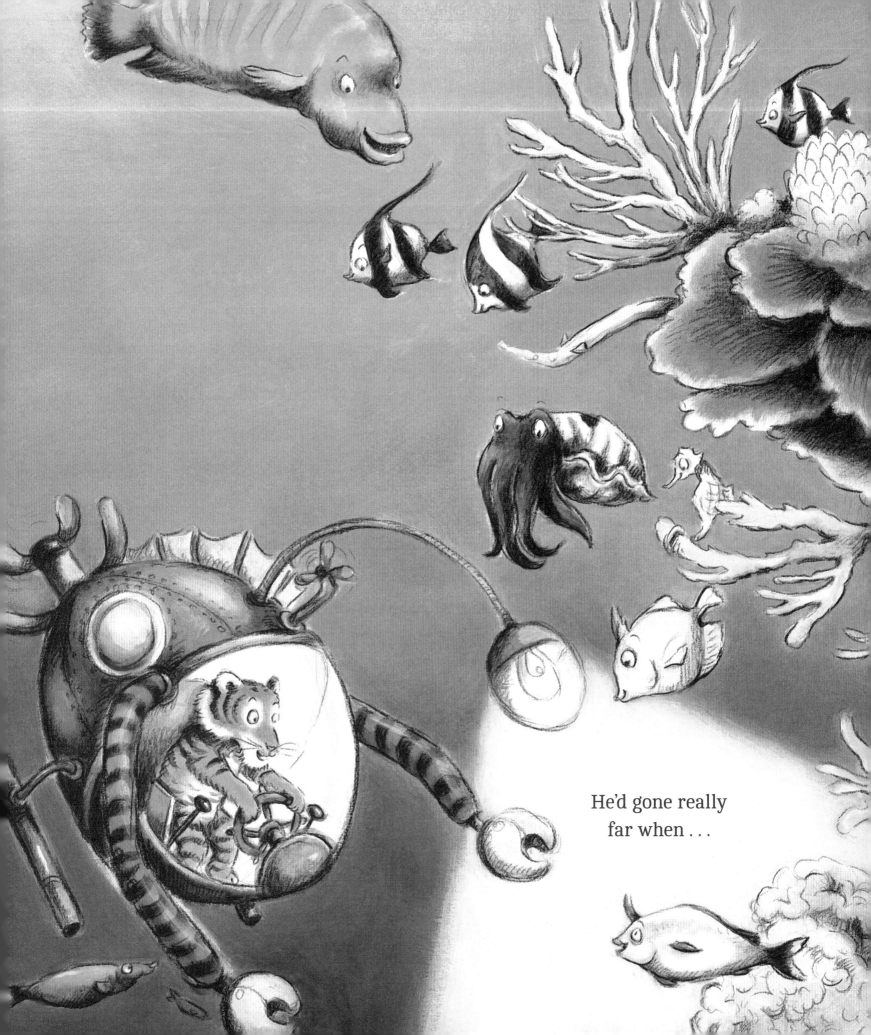

He'd gone really
far when . . .

Whoosh!

A whale swept him right back up to the surface!

"Never mind!" said Toby.
"I'm an **explorer**, and explorers
never give up!"

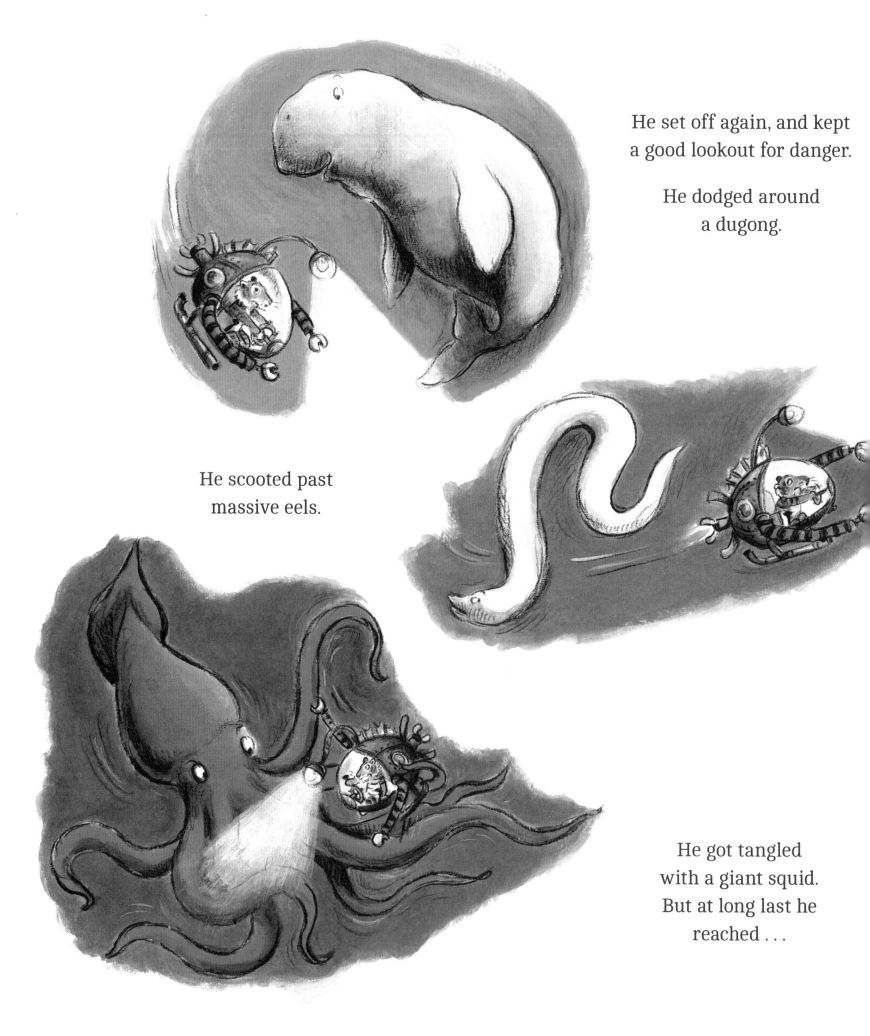

He set off again, and kept a good lookout for danger.

He dodged around a dugong.

He scooted past massive eels.

He got tangled with a giant squid. But at long last he reached . . .

. . . the Deep!

It was pitch dark,
and a little bit scary but . . .
Wow! What amazing creatures!

Toby gazed in astonishment.
He was the first tiger ever to see this.

He was photographing
everything and scribbling notes in
his diary when he spotted a commotion
down below. He could just see the bones of
a shipwreck – but what was that storm of
bubbles? A whirlpool? A sea monster?

Toby's heart beat fast as he inched towards it. To his surprise, he found . . .

. . . a turtle!

She was trapped in a fishing net,
and thrashing about in a panic. Toby knew
turtles could spend hours underwater, but they
have to come up for air sometimes. He'd have
to act fast if he was going to save her.

He revved his engine,
sped towards her
and clutched the net
with his grabber arms.

Then he pulled!

The net was really strong. The little submersible clanked and juddered. Toby was thinking he'd have to give up when he felt a

r-r-r-r-r-i-p!

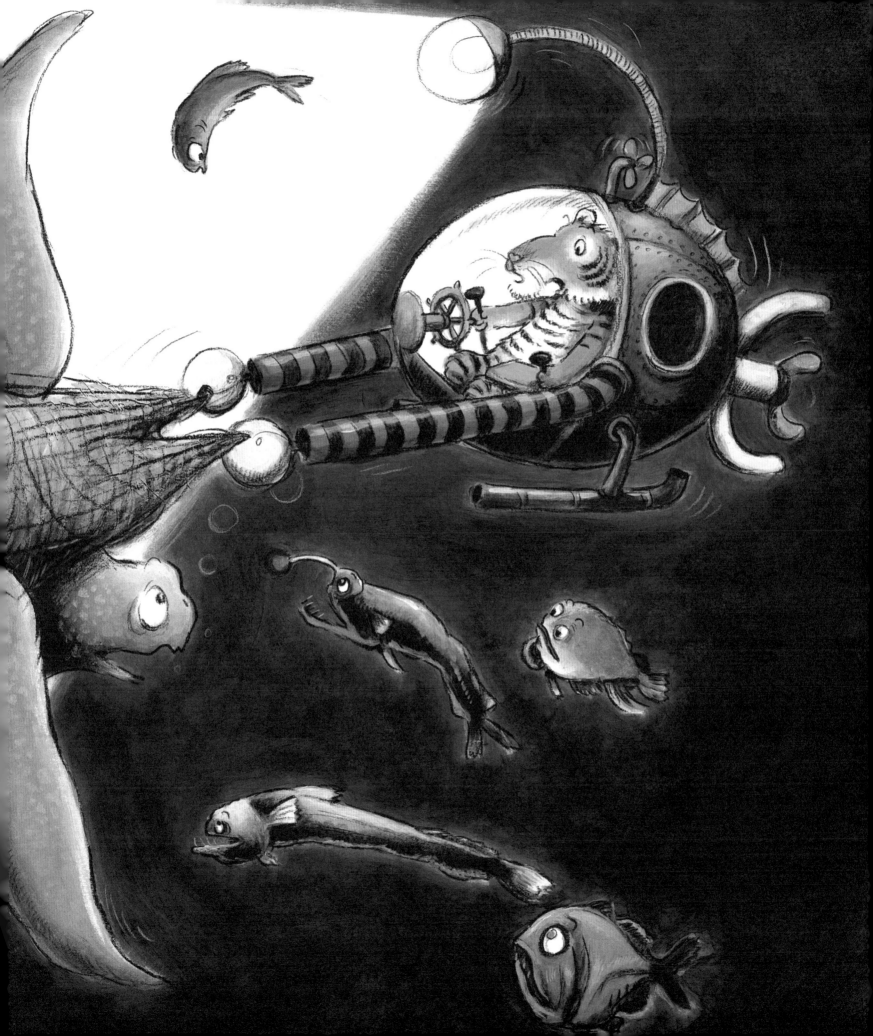

And the net tore apart!

The turtle was free!

It's not easy saying thank you underwater, but the
turtle grinned and waved her flippers for a photo.
Then she zoomed back up to the surface.
Toby waved happily. Then he
revved his engine again.

After all, there was still so much ocean to explore!

When Toby met the turtle, he saw the danger we cause to wildlife when we throw away rubbish like old fishing nets and plastic bags. Our oceans are an amazing, undiscovered wilderness. We've still only explored a tiny part of them, and have no idea how many extraordinary new creatures might be living down there!

Toby's story is inspired by some famous, real-life ocean explorers.

JACQUES COUSTEAU
(1910–1997)

INGENIOUS FRENCH EXPLORER AND INVENTOR

Like Toby, Jacques didn't train as a scientist, but he loved diving and longed to explore the ocean. To help him do that, Jacques joined forces with an engineer called Emile Gagnan.

Together they developed the Aqua-Lung, the world's first scuba-diving equipment. Now Jacques could really breathe underwater! He also helped invent a small submarine for exploring the ocean floor, and several underwater cameras.

Jacques loved sharing the wonders of the ocean with the world. He wrote over 50 books and made over 100 television programmes. But his greatest passion was the environment, and he never stopped striving to protect the world's oceans.

SYLVIA EARLE
(1935–)

RECORD-BREAKING AMERICAN OCEAN EXPLORER

When Sylvia first went scuba diving, she felt like she was flying underwater. She wanted to spend her life studying the ocean, but there weren't many female scientists in those days. At college, Sylvia was often the only woman in the whole class, but she never let that put her off.

Throughout her long career she has shown that women, as well as men, can be divers, researchers and scientists. She has spent over 7,000 hours underwater, and set a world record, diving 381m down to the ocean floor. Sylvia still works tirelessly to protect the oceans, and believes in treating all creatures with dignity and respect.

ERNEST EVERETT JUST
(1883–1941)

PIONEERING AFRICAN-AMERICAN BIOLOGIST

Not all explorers dive under the sea. Ernest Everett Just's explorations happened in a laboratory, where he studied small sea creatures and made exciting discoveries about the origins of life.

Ernest was a clever and dedicated student. He graduated at the top of his class and even qualified as a teacher at just 15 years old. However, his great passion was for scientific research. He was fascinated by sea creatures, and carried out careful, patient experiments, which helped him understand how their eggs developed. Despite suffering constant racial discrimination, Ernest made a huge contribution to biology. He is celebrated today as one of America's most important scientists.

For my lovely nephew,
Nathaniel Rentta

First published in the UK in 2021 by
Alison Green Books
An imprint of Scholastic Children's Books
Euston House, 24 Eversholt Street, London NW1 1DB
A division of Scholastic Ltd
www.scholastic.co.uk
London – New York – Toronto – Sydney – Auckland
Mexico City – New Delhi – Hong Kong
Designed by Zoë Tucker

HB ISBN: 978 0 702301 91 9
PB ISBN: 978 0 702301 92 6

Printed in Malaysia

1 3 5 7 9 8 6 4 2

Papers used by Scholastic Children's Books
are made from wood grown in sustainable forests.